THIS
BOOK BELONGS
TO ~~DINOSAURS~~
~~HUMANS~~
· · · · · · · · · · · · · · · · · ·

ORCHARD BOOKS

First published in 2019 by The Watts Publishing Group

First published in paperback in 2020

1 3 5 7 9 10 8 6 4 2

Text and illustrations © Matt Robertson 2019

The moral rights of the author and illustrator have been asserted. All rights reserved.

A CIP catalogue record for this book is available from the British Library.

HB ISBN 978 1 40835 157 4 • PB ISBN 978 1 40835 158 1

Printed and bound in China

Orchard Books

An imprint of Hachette Children's Group

Part of the Watts Publishing Group Limited

Carmelite House, 50 Victoria Embankment, London EC4Y 0DZ

An Hachette UK company

www.hachette.co.uk

www.hachettechildrens.co.uk

For Kitty and in memory of all the dinosaurs – M.R.

DINOSAURS vs HUMANS

Matt Robertson

ORCHARD

The **HUMANS** and the **DINOSAURS** had never got along. The Dinosaurs teased the Humans by singing silly songs . . .

But the naughty Humans, big and small,
would play their cheeky games,
Like tickling with feathers and
calling funny names.

In the middle of the squabble stood
a girl with bright pink hair.
PEARL didn't care for teasing and
she wished she was elsewhere.

DEXTER was a Dinosaur.

He hated all the fighting.

He wished he had a friend to take him

somewhere more exciting.

So while the tribes were busy warring,

little Dexter took a walk.
So did Pearl and –

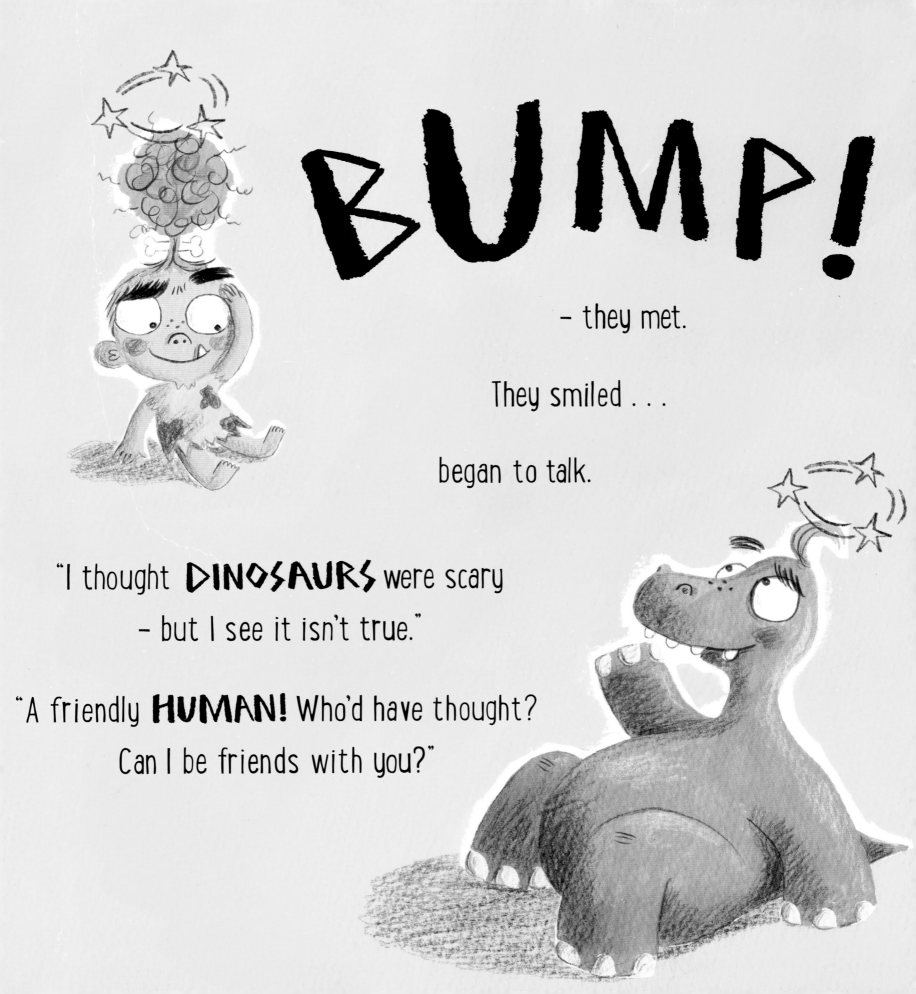

BUMP!

– they met.

They smiled . . .

began to talk.

"I thought **DINOSAURS** were scary
– but I see it isn't true."

"A friendly **HUMAN!** Who'd have thought?
Can I be friends with you?"

So Pearl and Dexter
LAUGHED

and
PLAYED,

they
JOKED
and
SHARED
their dreams.

And soon became the
BEST OF FRIENDS
– a Human–Dino team!

But their fun was always ruined by the others in the tribe:

HUMANS AND DINOSAURS MUST <u>NEVER</u> PLAY TOGETHER

"You **MUSTN'T** play together. It's against the Ancient Scribe."

But two determined, hopeful
friends will always find a way . . .

So they launched their
Great Escape Plan . . .

and found a
BRAND-NEW
place to play!

They explored the
MIGHTY JUNGLE,

every **CAVE**

and every **STREAM.**
Pearl and Dexter. Best of friends.
THE HUMAN-DINO TEAM!

But the distant fighting worsened and the trees began to **SHAKE**, Followed by a rumble that became a mighty **QUAKE**.

Then with the most almighty **CRACK**,

the ground beneath them **SPLIT**.

"**EEEK!**" screeched Dexter.

"**HELP!**" screamed Pearl . . .

"WE'RE TRAPPED INSIDE A PIT!"

The roaring tribes soon heard
their cries. They put down
stone and stick.

HEEEEE

EELLLLLLLLLP
"DEXTER!"
"PEARL!"
"In Danger."
"Where?"
"To the jungle!"
"QUICK!"

The humans got there first.
They STRETCHED into the pit.
They managed to get halfway down
but – oh dear! – that was it.

"Step aside, you useless lot.
Behold **OUR** strength and might."
The dinos **STRAINED** and **HAULED**
and **HEAVED**... but could they
reach? Not quite!

But then two voices floated up,
"You need to work TOGETHER.
Stop fighting and join forces –
or we'll be stuck down here for ever!"

The Humans and the Dinosaurs
looked over at their foes.

Then one by one they each took
hold of foot, or tail, or nose.

They put aside
their quarrels.

They were very
well behaved.

Their loved ones
both were SAVED!

The tribes felt rather sheepish.
How silly they had been!
For quarrelling and bickering
and always being mean.

"You dinos really aren't so bad.
In fact, you're rather smart."

"We **LOVE** your
silly human songs –
and your cool cave art."

So, thanks to Pearl and Dexter,
the two tribes now shook hands.
The war was finally over and peace
spread through their lands.

There was no more fighting. No more tricks.
No one bullied, teased or bitten.
Instead they found true friendship,
with the Ancient Laws . . .

rewritten.